RAINBOW magic ®

The Magical Animal Fairies

Join the **Rainbow Magic Reading Challenge!**

Read the story and collect your fairy points to climb the
Reading Rainbow at the back of the book.

This book is worth 5 points.

For Phoebe Graves,
with lots of love

Special thanks to
Sue Mongredien

ORCHARD BOOKS

First published in Great Britain in 2009 by Orchard Books
This edition published in 2016 by The Watts Publishing Group

1 3 5 7 9 10 8 6 4 2

© 2016 Rainbow Magic Limited.
© 2016 HIT Entertainment Limited.
Illustrations © Orchard Books 2009

HiT entertainment

A CIP catalogue record for this book is available from the British Library.

ISBN 978 1 40835 675 3

Printed in Great Britain

MIX
Paper from
responsible sources
FSC® C104740

The paper and board used in this book are made from wood from responsible sources

Orchard Books
An imprint of Hachette Children's Group
Part of The Watts Publishing Group Limited
Carmelite House, 50 Victoria Embankment, London EC4Y 0DZ

An Hachette UK Company
www.hachette.co.uk
www.hachettechildrens.co.uk

Sophia
the Snow Swan
Fairy

by Daisy Meadows

ORCHARD

There are seven special animals,
Who live in Fairyland.
They use their magic powers
To help others where they can.

A dragon, black cat, firebird,
A seahorse and snow swan too,
A unicorn and ice bear -
I know just what to do.

I'll lock them in my castle
And never let them out.
The world will turn more miserable,
Of that, I have no doubt...

Contents

Into the Darkness

Kirsty Tate bit into a warm, sticky
marshmallow and smiled. Bliss! It had
been another fantastic day at the
adventure camp where she and her best
friend, Rachel Walker, were staying for
a week. The sun was going down and
everyone was sitting around a fire,
singing songs and toasting marshmallows.
"I'm having such a brilliant holiday,"
Kirsty said happily to Rachel.

"Me too," Rachel agreed. Then she lowered her voice. "Especially with our new fairy friends!"

Kirsty smiled at her words. She and Rachel shared an amazing secret. They had met lots of fairies and had 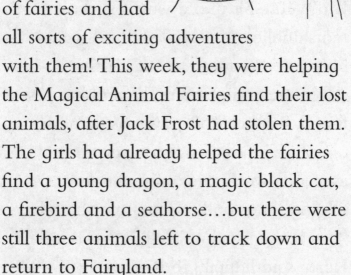 all sorts of exciting adventures with them! This week, they were helping the Magical Animal Fairies find their lost animals, after Jack Frost had stolen them. The girls had already helped the fairies find a young dragon, a magic black cat, a firebird and a seahorse...but there were still three animals left to track down and return to Fairyland.

"Listen up, guys!" said a voice just then. Kirsty and Rachel turned to see Trudi, one of the camp counsellors, standing on a tree stump. "There's such a wonderful full moon tonight, we're going to set off on a night hike. I've got something very special to show you all. Could you get into pairs, please?"

The campers immediately scrambled
to pair up. Kirsty and Rachel went
together, of course, and grinned at one
another. They always had their most
exciting adventures when it was just the
two of them!

Two other counsellors, Edward and
Lizzy, began passing out torches.
"Why are we going hiking in the dark
anyway?" a girl called Anna wanted
to know.

"Nature looks very different at night-time," Edward told her. "All kinds of birds and animals come out that you don't see in the day. And the surprise waiting for you at the end of the trail will definitely make the walk worth it!"

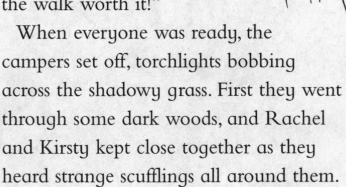

When everyone was ready, the campers set off, torchlights bobbing across the shadowy grass. First they went through some dark woods, and Rachel and Kirsty kept close together as they heard strange scufflings all around them.

Twigs cracked beneath their feet and Kirsty stumbled on a long, twisted root. It was a relief to come out from under the trees and into the open, where the moonlight shone silver on everything and lit the path ahead.

"It's so pretty," Rachel marvelled, as they walked alongside a bubbling stream. The moonlight glittered on the water as it rushed along.

"And look at that little swan!" Kirsty exclaimed. "It's so beautiful with the light reflecting on its white feathers – almost as if it were shimmering."

Rachel stared thoughtfully at the swan. The little bird did seem to be glowing in the darkness, its gleaming white feathers sending sparkling reflections into the water all around it.

"I think it *is* shimmering," Rachel whispered, clutching Kirsty and pulling her away from the path, so that the other campers could overtake. "Shimmering …as if it were magical!"

Kirsty felt her skin prickle with excitement, and she peered closely at the swan. "I think you're right," she said, when she and Rachel were alone. "That must be the Magical Snow Swan!"

Sophia Appears

The girls watched the little white swan as it sailed gracefully along the stream away from them, its neck curved in an elegant arch. They knew that the Magical Animals all possessed special powers, helping to spread the type of magic that every human and fairy can find within themselves: the magic of imagination, luck, humour, friendship, compassion, healing and courage.

The fairies trained the young animals for a whole year, teaching them how to use and control their powers. Once their training was complete, the Magical Animals returned to their families to spread their special gifts throughout Fairyland and the human world.

"The Magic Snow Swan spreads compassion," Rachel remembered. "That's when you are kind to someone who is sad or hurt, I think, and try to make them feel better."

"That *is* a lovely gift," Kirsty said. "Well,

we'll have to catch the swan somehow
and use our fairy dust to take her back
to Fairyland." She fingered the golden
locket that she always
wore around her
neck, which had
been given to
her by the
Fairy Queen
herself, and
was full
of magic
fairy dust.

"Good idea,"
Rachel agreed. "She
doesn't look as big as an ordinary,
fully grown swan, does she? Hopefully
we can scoop her up when she comes
near the bank."

The girls crept closer towards the stream. The swan was quite near to the grassy bank now and she dipped her head slightly to peck at some weed, the moonlight gleaming on her feathers. Kirsty took a deep breath and stepped forwards, arms outstretched. Her fingers were just about to touch the swan's white feathers when she trod on a twig, which cracked with a loud snapping sound.

The swan was startled and threw up her wings at once, splashing the water as she took off into the air. With just a few flaps, she had flown far upstream in fright.

"Oh no," Rachel groaned, watching the bird disappear. "Now what? Should we go to Fairyland anyway, to tell the fairies we've found the swan?"

"I—" Kirsty began, then stopped. "Rachel – look!" she said. "That flower in the grass. It's shining so brightly!"

Both girls stepped closer to the flower. It was a bright white, its closed petals glowing with light. Then, as Rachel and Kirsty watched, the flower petals opened…and a tiny fairy fluttered up into the air!

"Sophia!" Kirsty cheered, recognising
the Snow Swan Fairy. She and Rachel
had met all the Magical Animal Fairies
at the start of their adventure. Sophia
had long brown hair, fastened at one
side with a purple bow. She wore
a pinky-purple top dotted with
sparkles, and a fluffy pinky-
purple skirt. On her feet
were pretty purple
ballet shoes.

Sophia
did a
loop-the-
loop before
floating down to
hover in front of Kirsty and
Rachel. "Hello again, girls," she said
with a smile. "I came here because

I could sense my snow swan, Belle, was nearby. Have you seen her anywhere?"

"Yes," Rachel replied. "She was right here on the stream. But when we tried to catch her, she flew away into the distance!"

"You are so clever to have spotted her," Sophia said. "Now we need to find her again. Will you help me?"

"Of course," Kirsty said. "Let's—" But before she could finish her sentence, she heard the sound of footsteps approaching and she stopped speaking abruptly.

Kirsty and Rachel
turned to see Trudi
approaching, and
Sophia had to
dart out of sight
into one of
Kirsty's pockets
before she was spotted.

"Girls, what are you doing back here?"
Trudi exclaimed. "You must keep up –
we don't want anyone to get lost."

"Sorry," Rachel said, feeling guilty.
She'd been so excited about seeing Belle
the snow swan and Sophia that she'd
quite forgotten about the hike.

"Come on, let's catch up with the
others," Trudi said. "It won't be long
before we see the surprise – you can't
miss out on that!"

The girls followed Trudi along the trail and rejoined the group. Both felt rather subdued as the camp counsellor walked beside them. Kirsty could feel Sophia wriggling in her pocket and couldn't bear not to be able to talk about Belle and make plans to find her! What if the snow swan had flown far away? The chance to catch her would be lost!

The other campers were waiting on
a wider stretch of path. As Rachel and
Kirsty drew level with them, Rachel
noticed that Anna was looking confused.
"That's weird," she was saying to herself,
staring across the stream.

Rachel's heart quickened. What had
Anna seen? Had she caught a glimpse
of Belle the snow swan doing something
magical? "What's weird?"
she asked Anna.

"I thought I saw
a small green
creature on the
other side of
the stream,"
Anna replied,
rubbing her eyes
and staring again.

"Not a frog – bigger than that. And it was running on two legs – just like a little person!"

Rachel and Kirsty exchanged horrified glances, both thinking the same thing: it sounded as if Anna had just seen one of Jack Frost's sneaky goblins. The goblins would have been sent to look for Belle – so the girls had to find the snow swan fast!

Down the Waterfall

Anna shook her head and smiled. "The moonlight must be playing tricks on my eyes," she chuckled. "That – or some little green men have landed from Mars!"

Lucy, Anna's partner, giggled. "I don't think that's the surprise Trudi had lined up for us!" she said. "Come on, let's go."

Anna and Lucy set off together, and Kirsty turned to Rachel. "I bet it *was* a goblin," she murmured.

"Sounded like it to me," Sophia whispered from her hiding place. "We need to hurry!"

Kirsty and Rachel knew that Jack Frost had sent

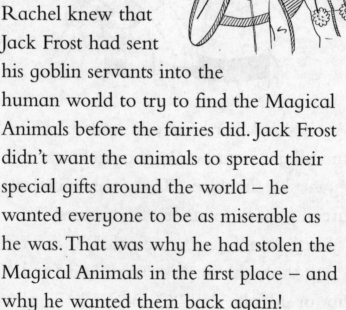

his goblin servants into the human world to try to find the Magical Animals before the fairies did. Jack Frost didn't want the animals to spread their special gifts around the world – he wanted everyone to be as miserable as he was. That was why he had stolen the Magical Animals in the first place – and why he wanted them back again!

Rachel and Kirsty scanned the
opposite side of the stream and all
around them as they went along, but
there was no sign of any goblins now.
Rachel could feel
goosebumps
rising along
her arms
as she
searched.
It was a bit
spooky, being
out at night,
wondering if a goblin was close by!

The stream soon widened and became
a river. After a few minutes' walking,
Kirsty suddenly grabbed Rachel's arm.
"Look," she said. "Straight ahead –
it's Belle!"

Sophia peeped over the edge of Kirsty's pocket and smiled in relief. "Yes, that's definitely her," she said in her silvery voice. "Now…let's think. I need to get her back without being seen."

Rachel bit her lip. "That's not going to be easy," she said in a low voice. "We can't hang back from the others again – Trudi will tell us off and may even take us back to camp. And I'm worried that if you fly across to Belle, Sophia, someone will spot you glittering in the darkness."

Sophia's pretty face twisted into a frown. "You're right," she said. "Anna already thinks she's seen a strange creature over there.

We can't risk her – or anyone else –
seeing *me*, too."

The three of them fell deep into
thought, watching Belle as she glided
serenely down the river. Then Kirsty
noticed that the river seemed to stop
dead further along, with the water
dropping over the edge. "It's a waterfall!"
she realised, open-mouthed.

The others looked. Kirsty was right. They could hear the water crashing down at the bottom of the waterfall, making a rushing, roaring sound as it tumbled over the rocks.

"There goes Belle!" Rachel whispered, trying not to stare too obviously as the beautiful white bird opened her wings again and took flight, soaring over the

edge of the waterfall. "Wow – you can hardly see her through all the spray."

It was true. They had reached the top of the waterfall now, and the cascades threw up such huge clouds of misty spray, that it was almost impossible to see the bottom from where they stood. Belle, too, had vanished into the mist.

"Can you all listen
to me for a moment?"
called Trudi just
then. "We're going
to work our way
down to the base
of the waterfall
now. There's a
path on your left
that we can follow
all the way. Take
your time, as some
of the rocks may
be wet and slippery."

"Is this the surprise?" one of the boys
called out curiously.

Trudi smiled. "We're nearly at the
surprise," she replied. "Just be patient and
all will be revealed! Let's go."

She led the group along a path that twisted and turned down the side of the waterfall. Sophia let out a little groan of frustration. "It's going to take ages to get down there," she sighed. "And Belle could fly miles away in that time. There's only one thing for it, girls – I'm going to have to turn you both into fairies. That way, we can all fly down together to the bottom of the waterfall, and find Belle."

She paused, and a flash of doubt crossed her face. "The only thing is, we must be careful not to fly too close to the waterfall. If our wings get wet from the spray, we won't be able to fly so well…which could be very dangerous."

Rachel and Kirsty exchanged a glance. It sounded rather nerve-racking, diving down to the bottom of the waterfall from such  a great height. But then a scuffling noise in the undergrowth nearby reminded them that there were goblins on the prowl – and they knew what they had to do.

"OK, let's do it," Kirsty said, looking around carefully to make sure that all the other campers and counsellors had started to make their way down the path. "Let's fly!"

An Icy Trap

Kirsty and Rachel hung back so that
they were at the tail end of the group
again. Then, when nobody was looking,
Sophia waved her wand over them,
sending streams of fairy sparkles whirling
around. The girls felt a familiar magical
tingle, and moments later they were
fairies, just like Sophia, with their own
glimmering wings that sparkled in the
moonlight.

"Ready? Then off we go!" Sophia called.

With a deep breath, Kirsty and Rachel plunged towards the heart of the waterfall, keeping a safe distance from the flying spray and making sure they kept out of sight of the rest of the group slowly making their way down the path.

"Whoaaaaa!" shouted Rachel. It was amazing – flying down so fast with the world blurring before her eyes. Kirsty was whooping alongside her, although it was hard to hear anything with the noise of the water tumbling below them.

It only took a few seconds for the three friends to reach the bottom – and then they all gasped as they saw what was there. Stretching through the mist was what looked like a dazzling white rainbow!

Kirsty and Rachel knew all about rainbows, of course, from their very first adventures with the Rainbow Fairies, but this was like no other rainbow they'd seen before. "I don't understand – how can there be a rainbow when it's so dark?" Rachel wondered in astonishment.

Sophia smiled. "It's a lunar rainbow – or a 'moonbow'," she explained. "They are very rare in the human world and only occur when the moon is at its fullest, and there is moisture in the air."

"Wow," Kirsty said, marvelling at the shining arc of light. "This must be what Trudi wanted to show us. This is the surprise!"

"And there's something even better," Rachel said, pointing excitedly. "I've just seen Belle!"

Kirsty and Sophia could also see the Magical Snow Swan gliding away from the waterfall on a new stretch of river. But unfortunately, they saw something else, too: three goblins on the river bank.

"Oh, no!" Kirsty exclaimed. "One of them has got a wand – where did he get that from?"

The goblin
pointed the
wand at the
river and the
three fairies watched in
dismay as a stream of icy
magic shot out from it, reaching
all the way to the snow swan, like
a jagged ice bridge.

"Jack Frost must have given them the
wand," Sophia realised. "And he's filled
it with his horrible icy magic."

Kirsty and Rachel felt alarmed. They
had seen the power of Jack Frost's magic
many times before – in particular when
they were helping the Petal Fairies.
The goblins had had a similar wand
then, which had caused all sorts of
problems for the girls.

The three goblins jumped onto the ice bridge and began skidding clumsily towards Belle.

"Quick, we've got to stop them," Sophia cried, fluttering forwards as fast as she could. Kirsty and Rachel flapped their gauzy wings hard as well,

zooming forwards at top speed. But they were too late. The goblins slid all the way over to Belle and waved the wand at her. There was a flash of electric-blue sparkles and then a cage made of icicles appeared around the snow swan. Belle was trapped!

The goblins chuckled with glee and did high-fives. The one nearest Belle picked up the ice cage and tucked it under one arm, before they all began sliding back towards the bank.

Belle's head drooped sadly. The cage was so small she couldn't even open her wings. She began to sing a mournful song that sent shivers down Kirsty's spine. "She sounds so unhappy," she said wretchedly.

Sophia nodded. "Belle's songs change according to how she's feeling," she said.

"When the Magical Snow Swans are very sad, they sing low and deep. When they are happy, they sing at a very high pitch – so high, in fact, that they can shatter glass." She smiled briefly. "Nobody in Fairyland minds, though, because they are always pleased to hear that a snow swan is happy."

"She's not happy now though, poor thing," Rachel said.

Sophia's smile vanished immediately. "No," she said. "She's not. We really must get her back from the goblins. I want to hear her singing happily again!"

Breaking Free

Rachel thought hard. "Can your magic melt the bars of the cage, Sophia?" she wondered.

Sophia nodded. "Yes, but we will need to get very close to the cage for it to work," she said. "Jack Frost's magic is always very powerful. The bars will probably be hard for me to break."

"Maybe we could distract the goblins.
Then you'll have a better chance of
flying near the cage," Kirsty suggested.

"Yes, we could buzz around their heads
like flies," Rachel put in. "They'll be so
busy trying to swat us, you'll be able to
sneak over to Belle."

Sophia smiled. "That's a great idea.
Let's try it!"

Rachel and Kirsty immediately flew
straight for the goblins and began darting
in front of their eyes, back and forth, up
and down, tickling their big ears
with their delicate
wings. "Get away
from me!" the
goblins grumbled,
lashing out at the
fairies. "Buzz off!"

The goblin with the cage was thrashing about so wildly he almost overbalanced on the icy bridge. He skidded forwards, bashing into the goblin in front – and then both of them landed on their bottoms.

Kirsty was having so much fun
annoying the goblins that she almost
forgot to watch what Sophia was doing.
Their fairy friend was close to the ice
cage now, shooting pink sparks at it from
her wand and dissolving the icicle bars
one by one. The plan was working!

But no sooner had the thought popped
into Kirsty's mind, than the goblin with
the wand seemed to lose all his patience
with Rachel – and zapped her with a
stream of icy magic!

Kirsty let out a scream
of horror as Rachel
froze solid and
plunged through the
air – heading
straight for the cold
water of the river!

Luckily, Sophia heard her cry out, and quickly pointed her wand at Rachel, sending a blast of fairy dust in her direction. Just as Rachel was about to hit the water, the fairy dust melted the ice around her, and she was able to flap her wings and soar up to safety. "Thank you!" she gasped breathlessly, her face pale with fright.

"Are you all right?" Kirsty asked, flying over to her. Sophia, too, left her position at the ice cage and fluttered up to Rachel.

"Quick, let's run!"
they heard the
goblins shout – and
turned to see the
three green figures
charging over the icy
bridge and back to the
riverbank. Then they vanished into
the shrubbery.

"After them!" Kirsty yelled, determined
not to let the goblins get away. She,
Rachel and Sophia flew over the river,
just as the icy bridge cracked and broke
into pieces. Seeing the ice gave Kirsty
an idea. "We have to make the ice cage
crack open!" she said as they flew.
"Sophia, didn't you say that a snow
swan's song can be high-pitched enough
to shatter glass? Maybe we can get her

song to shatter the ice around her!"

"Good thinking!" Sophia cried. "And
I know a way to make Belle sing in her
highest pitch. She and I have a little
game we play in Fairyland – I sing
the first part of a song and she
sings the second. It
always makes her
so happy that she ends
up singing very high!"

"Come on, then,
let's catch them up,"
Rachel said eagerly,
soaring through the air
as fast as she could.

It didn't take long before the
goblins were in sight. Sophia
launched into a melody at the top of her
voice, and they saw Belle lift her head

and turn towards
her mistress. The
swan opened her
beak and sang
back to Sophia,
making such a
high sound that
the girls covered
their ears!

Sophia sang another
melody, her silvery voice ringing
through the air.

Belle responded again, her voice
becoming higher and higher. It was so
high now that the goblin carrying the
cage had to put it down in order to hold
his hands over his ears. On and on Belle
sang, high and true – until the icicles
around her suddenly shattered!

"She did it!" Kirsty cheered, as the swan flapped her wings and took off into the air.

"Oh no, you don't!" the goblin yelled in alarm. He threw himself after Belle, his arms outstretched, and managed to grab her round the middle. "You're not going anywhere," he growled at her.

A Kind
Heart

Rachel felt her shoulders slump with
disappointment. Oh no! Their plan had
worked beautifully, too — how she wished
that Belle could have escaped!

Something very strange was happening,
though. Belle had turned her graceful
head so that she was looking straight
into the goblin's eyes, and began to sing

a new song. It was the most beautiful song the girls had ever heard — haunting and melodic, and full of emotion. Beside them, Sophia gave a sharp intake of breath. "Belle is singing the song of compassion!" she said. "A snow swan only ever sings this song if it senses that a person has compassion deep in their heart, which just needs to be unlocked."

"You mean…she thinks that the *goblin* has compassion inside him?" Kirsty asked in surprise. The goblins were mean and tricksy. They never usually showed kindness towards anybody!

64

"Let's watch and find out," Sophia said, her eyes glued to the goblin holding Belle.

The goblin was listening to the song as if bewitched. His face softened suddenly, and his eyes became kind. "You don't want to be a prisoner, do you?" he said softly to Belle, and then, in the next moment, opened his arms so that Belle could fly out of them.

Belle flew straight to Sophia, her neck stretched out like an arrow. As she flew, her body glittered all over with magical sparkles and she grew smaller and smaller, until she was her Fairyland size. She flew into Sophia's arms and the fairy gave her a delighted hug.

Meanwhile, the other goblins had been watching this in shock. "What were you playing at, letting the swan go?" one of

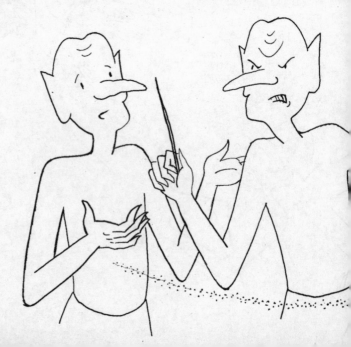

them raged, his hands on his hips. "If I'd known you were going to do that, I'd have used the wand to catch it again!"

The first goblin shrugged. "It just felt wrong to keep the swan when she wanted to be with her fairy mistress," he replied. "I'm proud of what I did – it was the right thing to do."

The third goblin snorted. "Well, Jack Frost won't think it was the right thing to do!" he argued. "He's going to be really angry!"

The first goblin was smiling at the sight of Sophia stroking Belle's soft feathers. "I don't think I want to work for Jack Frost anymore," he said. "Maybe I'll set up a Rescue Centre to help all the lost and lonely animals of Fairyland." And with that, he walked off, looking very happy.

The second goblin glared at Sophia and lifted his wand, as if about to cause mischief with it. Sophia was too quick for him, though. "If you try any more tricks, I'll get Belle to sing in a really high pitch again," she warned him. "Remember how that hurt your ears last time?"

The goblin looked stricken at the suggestion. "No more singing!" he begged. "My ears still hurt!" And he and the other goblin turned and ran away into the darkness.

"Just in time," Kirsty said as he vanished from sight. "I can hear the campers coming this way!"

Sophia gave Kirsty and Rachel a last hug. "Thank you," she said. "Now I'd better take Belle back with me to Fairyland, and turn you two into girls again." She waved her wand, and magical sparkles streamed all around Kirsty and Rachel.

Seconds later, they were girls once
more, and found themselves at the back
of the group of campers. They just
caught a glimpse of a bright speck of
light in the sky before it disappeared,
and knew Sophia was on her way to
Fairyland.

All around, the other campers were
exclaiming over the glittering lunar
rainbow that
spread across
the waterfall.

"It looks almost magical, doesn't it?" the girls heard Trudi saying, and they grinned at one another. Little did Trudi know all the magical things that had taken place down there just a few moments earlier!

"I love being friends with the fairies," Rachel whispered to Kirsty as they gazed at the rushing waterfall. "I do hope we have another fairy adventure soon!"

Now it's time for Kirsty and Rachel to help...

Leona the Unicorn Fairy

Read on for a sneak peek...

"Isn't this great, Kirsty?" Rachel Walker twisted round in her saddle to smile at her best friend, Kirsty Tate. "I'd only ever been horseriding once or twice before, but now I just love it!" And Rachel patted her chestnut pony, Sparkle.

"Me too," agreed Kirsty, who was on a beautiful black pony behind Rachel.

The girls had been having riding lessons ever since they arrived at camp, but this was the first time they'd been on a trail ride through the forest. "I think it's because Sparkle and Tansy are so sweet.

They don't mind if we do something wrong!"

"Keep following the trail, everyone," called Susan, their riding instructor, from the back of the line. There were several other campers on ponies in front of and behind Kirsty and Rachel. "It will lead us back to the camp eventually."

"I can't believe we've only got a day and a half left at camp," Rachel sighed as the ponies ambled on through the forest. It was cool and shady under the trees, but beams of sunlight dappled the grass here and there. "We've had *such* a good time, haven't we, Kirsty? We've tried hiking, orienteering, bird-watching and caving, and we've made some great friends."

But Kirsty wasn't really listening. She was staring around, peering through the trees on either side of the trail.

"Sorry, Rachel," she said quickly. "I was just seeing if I could spot anything unusual…"

Rachel smiled. She knew exactly what Kirsty was looking for! On the day the girls arrived at camp, the King and Queen of Fairyland had asked for their help. Kirsty and Rachel had discovered that Jack Frost and his goblin servants had kidnapped seven magical young animals from the Magical Animal Fairies…

Read Leona the Unicorn Fairy to find out what adventures are in store for Kirsty and Rachel!

Meet the
Friendship Fairies

When Jack Frost steals the Friendship Fairies' magical objects, BFFs everywhere are in trouble! Can Rachel and Kirsty help save the magic of friendship?

www.rainbowmagicbooks.co.uk

Calling all parents, carers and teachers!
The Rainbow Magic fairies are here to help
your child enter the magical world of reading.
Whatever reading stage they are at, there's
a Rainbow Magic book for everyone!
Here is Lydia the Reading Fairy's guide to
supporting your child's journey at all levels.

①

Starting Out
Our Rainbow Magic Beginner Readers are perfect for first-time readers who are just beginning to develop reading skills and confidence. Approved by teachers, they contain a full range of educational levelling, as well as lively full-colour illustrations.

②

Developing Readers
Rainbow Magic Early Readers contain longer stories and wider vocabulary for building stamina and growing confidence. These are adaptations of our most popular Rainbow Magic stories, specially developed for younger readers in conjunction with an Early Years reading consultant, with full-colour illustrations.

③

Going Solo
The Rainbow Magic chapter books - a mixture of series and one-off specials - contain accessible writing to encourage your child to venture into reading independently. These highly collectible and much-loved magical stories inspire a love of reading to last a lifetime.

www.rainbowmagicbooks.co.uk

"Rainbow Magic got my daughter reading chapter books. Great sparkly covers, cute fairies and traditional stories full of magic that she found impossible to put down" - Mother of Edie (6 years)

"Florence LOVES the Rainbow Magic books. She really enjoys reading now" - Mother of Florence (6 years)

The Rainbow Magic Reading Challenge

Well done, fairy friend – you have completed the book!
This book was worth 5 points.

See how far you have climbed on the
Reading Rainbow opposite.

The more books you read, the more points you will get,
and the closer you will be to becoming a Fairy Princess!

How to get your Reading Rainbow
1. Cut out the coin below
2. Go to the Rainbow Magic website
3. Download and print out your poster
4. Add your coin and climb up the Reading Rainbow!

There's all this and lots more at
www.rainbowmagicbooks.co.uk

You'll find activities, competitions, stories, a special
newsletter and complete profiles of all the
Rainbow Magic fairies. Find a fairy with your name!